For Longiswa, my Kwela Jamela

Copyright © 2001 by Niki Daly

By arrangement with The Inkman, Cape Town, South Africa

Hand-lettering by Andrew van der Merwe

First published in Great Britain by Frances Lincoln Limited, 2001

Printed in Singapore

First American edition, 2001

1 3 5 7 9 10 8 6 4 2

Library of Congress Cataloging-in-Publication Data

Daly, Niki.
    What's Cooking, Jamela? / story and pictures by Niki Daly.—1st American ed.
        p. cm.
    Summary: Jamela is responsible for fattening up the chicken intended for Christmas
dinner, but instead she gives it a name and makes it her friend.
    ISBN 0-374-35602-5
    [1. Chickens—Fiction.   2. Christmas—Fiction.   3. Blacks—South Africa—Fiction.   4.
South Africa—Fiction.] I. Title.

PZ7.D1715 Wh 2001
[E]—dc21

00-63618

What's Cooking, Jamela?

STORY
+ PICTURES by
NiKi DALY

FARRAR, STRAUS & GIROUX
New York

Gogo and Mama were making plans for Christmas.

"I'll make the pudding. You can do a chicken," said Gogo.

"And Thelma will cook a nice rice and *marogo* stew," said Mama.

"Good," said Gogo. "We'll have a lovely Christmas meal."

Jamela knew all about Christmas. It was a time to celebrate baby Jesus' birthday with a nativity play at school. Christmas also meant Christmas presents and getting together with the family.

When Gogo left, Mama said, "Come, Jamela, let's go to Mrs. Zibi and buy one of her young chickens. If we feed it well, it will be nice and fat for Christmas."

Mama let Jamela choose the chicken— a beautiful red one. Mrs. Zibi gave them a bag of *mielies*.

"We can call her Christmas," said Jamela. Mama laughed. "That's a good name for a Christmas chicken, Jamela."

When they got home, Mama showed Jamela how much water and *mielies* the chicken would need every day.

"See if she will eat out of your hand," suggested Mama.
Nervously, Jamela held out a handful of yellow *mielies*.

"Look, Mama, she's eating!" squealed Jamela.

"Now it's time to feed my own chick," said Mama, smiling.

Before she went to bed, Jamela asked, "How long until Christmas, Mama?"

"When our chicken is nice and fat, then it will be Christmas," replied Mama.

Every morning before school, Jamela gave Christmas food and water. If there was time, she let Christmas sit in her lap and hand-fed her *mielies*.

That bird just loved to eat! Mama scooped up the chicken droppings, which she used to make fertilizer to feed her squashes. Every day the chicken and the squashes seemed to grow rounder and larger.

Whenever Gogo visited, she asked, "How is our Christmas meal doing?" Jamela frowned and said, "She's doing fine, Gogo." But she didn't like the way Gogo licked her lips—like the lady on the fried-chicken TV commercial.

At school, they did a nativity play. There were angels and
African dancers. Jamela played Mary and carried baby Jesus on her
back like a real mama. Vuyo was a very handsome Joseph in his
Basuto hat and blanket.

Tabu, Elliot, and Zingi were splendid Wise Men in their Madiba shirts.

They sang "Away in a Manger" and other Christmas songs to the sound of marimba and drums. Everyone clapped and sang along.

When Jamela and Mama got home, Jamela made a manger for Christmas.

"That's a lovely manger, but I hope you're not growing too fond of that chicken," said Mama.

"No, Mama," sang Jamela, as she ran outside calling, "Christmas! Chick, chick—come and see what I've made for you!"

Mama was worried when she saw how happy Jamela and the big fat chicken looked, sitting side by side. Just how would she get the chicken away from Jamela and into a pot?

The day before Christmas, Mrs. Zibi came round.

"Jamela, please go and see how Thelma is getting on with the rice and *marogo*," said Mama.

Jamela looked at Mrs. Zibi's big hands as they rubbed against her apron. They looked ready for serious business.

"Stop staring and go now, Jamela," said Mama.

Jamela knew it was bad manners to argue with grownups, but she didn't like the look of things.

"Okay, Mama," said Jamela, as she set off to Thelma's house . . .

. . . with Christmas in her arms.

Christmas flapped and squawked. She almost flew out of Jamela's arms.

"Do you want to sell that chicken?" called a lady who was cooking chicken legs for her customers.

Jamela shook her head—"*Aikona!*"—and hurried along.

"Toot! toot!" a taxi hooted. Startled, Jamela jumped, and let go of Christmas. Laughter filled the taxi stand as the chicken scrambled between legs and disappeared into the crowd.

"Christmas, chick chick!" wailed Jamela. But Christmas was nowhere to be seen. Gone!

Jamela walked slowly home. At the end of her street, she saw
Mama and Mrs. Zibi running toward her. Mama looked worried.
Mrs. Zibi looked cross. How Jamela wished she could grow wings
and fly over their heads, down the street and far, far away.

"Where's the chicken?" panted Mrs. Zibi.

Jamela flapped her arms weakly. "Gone," she said.

"Oh, Jamela!" sighed Mama.

Jamela looked sorry—but inside, she was smiling. Wherever Christmas was, she was not in anyone's pot!

Mama took Jamela firmly by the hand, and they walked home. When they passed Archie, Mama greeted him. "*Molo*, Archie. Have you seen our chicken?"

"*Aikona*," replied Archie. "But if I do, I'll tell it that you ladies are looking for it."

Down the road, old Greasy Hands was revving up a car.

"*Molo*, Greasy Hands!" shouted Mama over the noise.

"Have you seen our chicken?"

"Whaaat?" shouted Greasy Hands.

Just then, a taxi skidded to a stop.

The passengers shouted, "*Hamba!* Get it out, get it out!"
The taxi door opened, and out jumped a plump red chicken.
Christmas fluffed out her feathers, then took off—over the
pavement and into Miss Style hairdressers.
"Quick, quick!" shouted Mama.

Inside the salon, Christmas was running wild over counters and half-braided ladies. Hair dryers, shampoo, combs, braids, and beads went flying.

Mama grabbed a basket and cornered Christmas.

"*VIVA!*" shouted the ladies
when Mama managed to throw
the basket over the frantic chicken.

Mrs. Zibi thrust her hands under the basket and pulled out
Christmas. "From the basket to the pot!" she hollered.

"Oh, Mama, Mama! Please don't let Mrs. Zibi hurt Christmas!"
cried Jamela.

"A chicken is a chicken!" snapped Mrs. Zibi.

"Christmas is not a chicken," cried Jamela. "Christmas is my friend. And you can't eat friends."

Mama looked at the ladies for help. But the ladies were all smiling sweetly at Jamela.

"You can't eat friends," echoed the ladies.

"*Ga*, nonsense!" scolded Mrs. Zibi.

On Christmas morning, Jamela helped Mama prepare their
Christmas meal. The rich chicken fertilizer had given the squashes
soft, succulent flesh. Jamela scooped out the seeds and put them
aside. Mama filled the hollow with a mixture of nuts, bread crumbs,
butter, and tasty herbs.

By the time Gogo and the other family members arrived,
mouth-watering smells filled the kitchen.

Gogo sniffed and asked, "What's cooking, Jamela?"

"It's a surprise, Gogo," Jamela replied.

After everyone had exchanged presents, Mama invited the family to the table and served the food. Steam danced around Thelma's rice and *marogo* stew. Mama took the lid off the delicious-smelling baked squash.

Jamela could see Gogo's eyes searching for the chicken. But Gogo didn't say anything. Everyone was happy to be enjoying a Christmas dinner together.

After the dessert, Gogo rubbed her tummy. Then, looking at Mama, she said, "*Haai!* That was better than a five-star hotel. But, *sisi*, where is the chicken?"

Jamela jumped up from the table.

"I'll show you, Gogo," she said. Grabbing Gogo's hand, she led her out into the yard, where Christmas was enjoying a tasty feast of squash seeds.

"Look, Gogo—there's the chicken!" said Jamela. "Mama has given her to me for a Christmas present. Her name is Christmas."

Gogo looked at the beautiful chicken, but she didn't lick her lips. Instead, she hugged Jamela against her full tummy and said, "Well, it looks like a very happy Christmas to me."

You bet!

Glossary

Aikona (Xhosa and Zulu): No!

Basuto: The people of Lesotho (formerly Basutoland)

Ga (Afrikaans): An exclamation of disgust

Gogo (Xhosa and Zulu): A term of respect for elderly women, commonly used to address grandmothers

Haai (Xhosa): An exclamation of surprise

Hamba (Nguni): Go away! Shoo!

Madiba (Xhosa): Clan name of the Tembu chiefdom. The name Madiba is applied affectionately to Nelson Mandela, a noble member of the Madiba clan and the first black president of South Africa. Fashion followers in South Africa refer to beautiful shirts with ethnic patterns as "Madiba shirts," after Madiba, who wears them with so much style

Marimba (possibly Swahili): African xylophone

Marogo (Sotho): Green vegetable leaves used for cooking

Mielies (Afrikaans): Corn

Molo (Xhosa): Hello

Sisi (Xhosa): Sister. African women are addressed as "sisi" (except older women, who are called "mama"). A mother calls her daughter "sisi" as an endearment

Viva: Portuguese victory salute found in Angola and Mozambique, now used as a cry of celebration